ANIMAL
EMERGENCY

BAD LUCK
LION

BAD LUCK
LION

EMILY COSTELLO

ILLUSTRATED BY LARRY DAY

AN AVON CAMELOT BOOK

This is a work of fiction. Names, characters, places, and incidents either are the product of the author's imagination or are used fictitiously. Any resemblance to actual events, locales, organizations, or persons, living or dead, is entirely coincidental and beyond the intent of either the author or the publisher.

AVON BOOKS, INC.
1350 Avenue of the Americas
New York, New York 10019

Copyright © 1999 by Emily Costello
Interior illustrations copyright © 1999 by Avon Books, Inc.
Interior illustrations by Larry Day
Published by arrangement with the author
Library of Congress Catalog Card Number: 98-94858
ISBN: 0-380-79755-0
www.avonbooks.com

First Avon Camelot Printing: August 1999

CAMELOT TRADEMARK REG. U.S. PAT. OFF. AND IN OTHER COUNTRIES, MARCA REGISTRADA, HECHO EN U.S.A.

Printed in the U.S.A.

OPM   10   9   8   7   6   5   4   3   2   1

For Becky and Sierra

"Find any?" Stella Sullivan called to her father.

"Not yet," Jack called back. His voice was softened by the forest that surrounded them.

It was a sunny Thursday afternoon. Perfect for mushroom hunting. Nine-year-old Stella, her father and her grandfather had been in the woods for half an hour. So far Papa Pete was the only one who had found any mushrooms.

"Here's some more!" Papa Pete shouted.

"Show off," Stella muttered to herself.

Papa Pete sank to his knees and began plucking mushrooms out of the moist soil. He deposited them into a plastic bag. While he was bent over, Stella could see the top of his head. The bald spot was ringed with a fringe of snow-white hair.

Stella slowly turned in a circle, looking up at the cottonwood trees. It was early May in Montana. Shiny green leaves had just started to poke out of cottonwood buds. Stella spotted a fallen tree a dozen yards away. Papa Pete told her rotting wood created rich soil that mushrooms loved.

"Come on, boy!" Stella tugged gently on her puppy's leash and started toward the downed tree.

Rufus was twelve weeks old, and he didn't much like being told where to go. The puppy was having an extra hard time obeying that afternoon. He'd discovered that the woods were full of interesting smells. As they walked, Rufus excitedly sniffed at the leaves and twigs, pulling Stella this way and that way.

Stella wondered if Rufus had ever been in the woods before. She wasn't sure because she didn't know much about the puppy's early life. He'd been abandoned at a rest stop when he was just a few weeks old. Stella wasn't even certain of his breed. He had a white coat, a black nose and lips, and a pink tongue. People said he looked like a Maltese. He had grown to the size of a soccer ball.

When they got to the fallen tree, Stella gently pulled back on the leash. "Whoa," she said. "Let's see if there are any mushrooms under here."

Rufus sat, panting happily.

Stella peered under the tree. She spotted a tall,

skinny mushroom sprouting out of the damp ground.

"I've got one!" Stella hollered. She put down Rufus's leash so that she could pluck it.

As Stella popped the mushroom into her bag, Rufus let out a high-pitched bark and lunged forward. He bounded through the trees with his leash trailing after him.

"Rufus! Come back!" Stella called.

A red squirrel darted through the fallen leaves. Rufus was in hot pursuit. The squirrel scurried up a tree. Rufus ran to the base of the trunk.

"Ruf! Ruf, ruf, ruf!"

Papa Pete slowly approached Rufus from behind. He grabbed the puppy's leash and gave it a firm yank. "No!" he said in a deep, barklike tone.

Rufus sat and lowered his head.

Stella rushed over. She snatched the leash out of Papa Pete's hand. "You didn't have to yell at him!" she exclaimed.

"Oh, yes I did!" Papa Pete told her with a little laugh. His brilliant blue eyes were set in a deeply tanned face—an outdoorsman face.

"He's just a puppy!" Stella shot back.

Papa Pete frowned, and the creases in his forehead deepened. "That little rat is old enough to learn some manners," he said gruffly. "And *you're* old enough to know better than to sass me."

Stella's mouth dropped open. Her grandfather had called Rufus a *rat*. He had no right! She had to bite her tongue to stay quiet.

Papa Pete thought children shouldn't talk back to grown-ups. Stella knew that if she argued with him, he'd give her a long lecture. Sometimes Stella couldn't even believe she was related to Papa Pete. Or that Papa Pete was Jack's father. The two men were so different.

Stella's dad was funny. He loved to cook and spend time with people.

Papa Pete lived alone in the log cabin he'd built in the hills above town.

Jack loved animals almost as much as Stella did.

But Papa Pete was a hunter. He enjoyed nothing more than camping out in the woods with his dogs and his guns. People paid him money and he helped them track and shoot wild animals. Stella hated to think about it.

Jack came up and put a comforting hand on Stella's shoulder. "Looks like we have plenty of mushrooms for a super spaghetti sauce," he said.

"Then let's head back," Papa Pete said, still looking angry. "I don't want to keep you from your pots and pans."

"We have plenty of time." Jack easily ignored Papa Pete's unpleasant tone. "What do you say we work up an appetite? We could take a hike up the mountain. I know a trail that passes near here."

"Sure!" Stella agreed. Hiking was one of her favorite things. And her dog-training book said puppies should be exposed to new experiences. Exploring the woods would be good for Rufus.

"Lead the way," Papa Pete said to Jack. Anyone who'd ever hiked with Stella's dad knew he belonged out in front. He could move fast.

Jack stowed the bag of mushrooms in his backpack. Then he began to make his way through the trees. Rufus and Stella followed, with Papa Pete right behind them. Jack found the trail and picked up his pace even more.

Stella calmed down as she made her way over the roots and rocks on the trail. Rufus trotted along with his nose to the leaves and dirt.

Occasionally the path passed over small stream beds which were fed by snow melting higher in the mountains. Stella crossed the streams by carefully stepping from one exposed rock to the next. Rufus splashed right through. His legs were soon splattered with mud.

After twenty minutes, the trail began to lead up the mountainside. The ground turned dry and gravelly. The cottonwoods gave way to an aspen grove. Long, brown catkins decorated the trees— but the leaves hadn't come out yet.

"Stella," Papa Pete said quietly. They had just reached the edge of the aspens and were following the trail into a small meadow. Jack had already passed through the meadow and into the stand of spruce trees beyond.

"What?"

"Shh," Papa Pete whispered. "Look." He came up beside her and pointed.

The light was beginning to fade. At first, Stella didn't see anything.

"I don't—" Stella started. Then something moved near the far edge of the meadow. Suddenly, Stella could see several large mule deer peacefully nibbling on the new grass. They were bucks with large branched antlers and oversized ears. The front of their muzzles was black. Their legs looked too slender to carry their solid bodies.

"Nice," Stella said, breaking into a smile. She watched the deer for several minutes, pleased that Rufus stood quietly at her side.

"Come on," Papa Pete said. "Your dad's probably on top of the mountain by now."

Stella stepped forward.

But Rufus refused to move. He hunkered down and let out a low growl.

"What is it, boy?" Papa Pete whispered.

Stella grew still. She looked in the direction Rufus was gazing so intensely.

The deer stopped eating. They raised their heads at the same time and seemed to strain for a sound or a smell. Then—as if following some silent signal—they all startled and bounded off together.

Stella spied something that looked like a shadow racing gracefully through the undergrowth. She caught a glimpse of a silver-tan coat. Big paws. A tail—a massive tail. A lanky gallop. Her mind put the fleeting impressions together.

A mountain lion!

By the time Stella knew what she was seeing, the deer and lion were gone. "That was so cool!" she exclaimed. "I've never seen a mountain lion before. I mean, I've seen them in zoos, but never out in the wild!"

"Did you notice her spots?" Papa Pete asked calmly. He was smiling ever so slightly.

"No."

"Baby cougars have spots until they're about nine months old," Papa Pete said.

"Nine months . . . Do you think her mother is still around?"

"Nah. Cat that age is probably out trying to find territory of her own. A hunting ground she can call home."

"Do you think she caught one of those deer?"

Papa Pete shot her a surprised look. "I thought you *saw* that lion."

"I did!"

"Didn't you notice her face was full of quills?" Papa Pete asked.

"Porcupine quills?"

Stella's Aunt Anya was a veterinarian, and Stella spent most of her free time hanging out at her animal clinic. Dogs often came into the clinic after losing a fight with a porcupine. Stella had seen dozens of dogs having quills removed from their tongues, gums, and faces. Pulling out all of the long needlelike quills took patience, but it wasn't difficult. And the dogs were *so* grateful.

Papa Pete nodded abruptly and started to walk.

"Wait!" Stella said. "We have to do something."

"Nothing to do. With her mouth full of barbs, that cat will starve."

Stella shuddered, imagining a bunch of quills in the cat's tongue. Eating would drive them in farther. Even closing her mouth might hurt. She stared into the underbrush where the mountain lion had disappeared, wishing she could think of some way to help her.

Papa Pete stopped on the other side of the meadow and motioned for her to follow. "Forget about that cat. She's as good as dead."

"No, she's not," Stella told him. "I'm going to save her."

Jack was waiting for Stella and Papa Pete a few hundred yards into the woods. Stella quickly talked her father and grandfather into heading home. She was anxious to tell her mom about the injured mountain lion.

Stella's mom—Norma Sullivan—was a wildlife biologist. She worked in Goldenrock, a huge national park. Norma was an expert on wild animals. She would know what to do to help the lion.

Rufus led the way down the mountain, with Stella at the other end of the leash. Papa Pete and Jack were walking together. They fell behind.

Stella was relieved when the trail leveled out and the forest changed back to cottonwood. They were almost to her father's truck.

She was crossing a shallow creek when Rufus suddenly pulled sideways. Stella didn't want him to get too far away from her. She didn't need him chasing more squirrels.

"Rufus . . . stop," Stella called.

The little dog splashed downstream as far as his leash would let him. He lowered the front of his body and barked. Stella had never heard him make a sound like that before. The bark was deep and mixed with a throaty growl.

"Shh, Rufus," Stella said. "What's the matter with you?"

Rufus's violent barking scared her. Could he be hurt? The thought sent her splashing after him. Stella was several yards out into the stream when she saw a spotted fawn lying in the middle of the water.

"Oh," Stella said, instantly freezing.

The fawn's big soft eyes were focused on Rufus. Her ears and nose twitched nervously. She struggled to get to her feet—but something pulled her back down with a splash.

Rufus was still barking. Stella was shaking as she scooped him up and carried him to dry land. She took him several yards down the trail and tied his leash to a tree. Then she backtracked to the stream.

Moving slowly and murmuring softly, Stella

approached the fawn. It bleated, scooting away from Stella but not running off. Stella felt unsettled. Something was wrong. Wild animals don't usually let you approach them without running away.

When she got a little closer, Stella could see why the fawn didn't dash into the woods. One of her delicate hind legs was caught in something shiny. *A trap,* Stella thought with an awful, sinking feeling. The fawn's leg was raw and red where the steel teeth had broken her skin. Her fur was matted with blood. Tears sprang to Stella's eyes, but she angrily blinked them back.

"Stella? What's happening?"

Jack and Papa Pete had finally made their way down the mountain. They were standing together in the middle of the stream, looking down at Stella.

"Some stupid hunter abandoned a trap," Stella said angrily.

"Trapping season is over," Papa Pete said.

"I know!" Stella shouted. Trapping wasn't allowed in the spring because so many baby animals were born then. "I bet the trapper knew, too," Stella went on. "But he was too lazy to come pick up his traps. Obviously, he didn't care if a baby animal got caught."

"You don't know that," Papa Pete said.

"Can we do something?" Jack knew even less about animal medicine than Stella. He taught journalism at Montana State University.

Stella took a deep breath and tried to think. "The fawn's leg may be broken. We need to make a splint. What do we have with us?"

"Nothing." Papa Pete held up his hands.

But Jack hopped over to the stream bank, took off his backpack, and put it down. He unzipped it, pulled out the bags of mushrooms, and peered inside. "Water bottle, compass, map, flashlight, last month's *Montana* magazine—"

"I can use that." Stella stood up, unbuckled her belt, and slid it off. "I'm going to need help releasing the trap. Then someone will need to hold the fawn down while I put the splint on."

"No problem," Jack said.

Papa Pete made an impatient noise.

The fawn's eyes were wide with fear, but she'd quit struggling. Stella wasn't sure if that was a good sign or a bad one. Could the shock of being so close to humans scare her to death?

Stella took off the long-sleeved shirt she was wearing over her T-shirt. She crept forward and tossed the shirt over the animal's head. At least now the fawn couldn't see them. That should help her calm down.

"May I have your shirt, too, Daddy?" Stella asked.

"Sure." Jack removed his shirt and handed it to Stella. She put it down on a clear patch of ground. "Ready when you are," she said.

"I'll do the trap," Jack said. "You hold on to her."

Stella nodded.

They approached the fawn slowly. Stella got down on her hands and knees in the shallow water. She wrapped one arm around the fawn just under her throat. Then she gently leaned her weight against the animal's body. The fawn was about the size of a collie dog, but much slighter in build.

"Ready?" Jack asked.

Stella nodded.

Jack reached into the water and popped the trap open. The fawn began to thrash. Jack quickly moved in, getting one hand around the fawn's neck and the other around her hind legs.

Jack stood up clumsily. Stella's shirt still covered the fawn's head.

"Careful, Jack," Papa Pete warned. "Those hooves are sharp."

"Thanks!" Jack turned his face away from the fawn's tiny hooves.

"Put her down on your shirt," Stella said.

Jack carefully made his way out of the stream.

He laid the fawn down on her side, holding her there with his forearms.

Stella forced herself to look at the fawn's bloody leg. A white patch of bone was visible just above the hoof.

"Oh, Daddy . . ." Stella breathed. She closed her eyes, feeling her stomach do a slow turn.

"Muffin? Are you okay?"

"Yes," Stella said quickly. She took a deep breath and rolled the magazine around the fawn's leg—hiding the rawest part. She coiled her belt around the magazine, pulled it tight, and tucked the ends under.

"Nice work." Jack gave Stella an encouraging nod.

"Thanks." Stella sighed with relief—the worst was over.

"Now what?" Papa Pete asked impatiently.

"We take her back to the clinic so Anya can work on her," Stella said.

"That's ridiculous." Papa Pete shook his head, looking disgusted.

Stella felt the blood rush to her face. She sat up straighter and glared at Papa Pete. "Why?" she demanded.

"You've got some romantic idea that this baby deer needs your help," Papa Pete said. "But that's a wild critter. She's not going to like being carried out of the woods. And she'll probably be trouble in the car. Maybe even cause an accident. Too dangerous."

Stella gave her father a pleading look. A fawn with a broken leg would never survive in the wild. They *couldn't* just leave the fawn there to die.

"Now, don't worry, Dad," Jack said soothingly. "Norma is always dragging some wild critter out of the woods. We hauled home an otter a few weeks back. I think we can make the trip safely."

Stella felt a surge of hope. "We could tie up the fawn's legs so she won't kick," she suggested. "And I'll hold her in the backseat while we ride into town. With my shirt over her head, she should be pretty calm."

Papa Pete didn't look convinced. "What are you going to use to tie her up?"

For a moment, Stella was stumped. But her mind seemed to be working double-time. "We could use Rufus's leash," she suggested.

"Good idea," Jack said.

Stella didn't give her grandfather time to disagree. She ran down the trail to where she had left the puppy.

Rufus had given up barking and was lying under a tree with his head on his paws. As Stella approached, he slowly got to his feet and gave her a resentful look.

Stella had to laugh. "I'm sorry you missed all the excitement," she told him. "But you were scaring the poor fawn."

She led Rufus down the trail. When she got close to her father, she picked up the dog, unhooked his leash, and tossed it to her dad.

Jack was still close to the ground, holding down the fawn. "I'm going to need some help," he grunted.

Papa Pete motioned to Stella with a couple of fingers. "I'm too old to wrestle with wild animals," he said. "Give me the dog."

Stella hesitated for a split second before realizing she had no choice. Without the puppy's leash, she couldn't tie him up. She handed Rufus to her grandfather and went to help her father. Jack tied the leash around the fawn's three good legs—the same way a cowboy would "hog-tie" a calf. Then he gently picked up the fawn and headed down the trail.

"Let's go!" he called.

Stella grabbed the backpack. Papa Pete held on to Rufus. The three of them moved down the trail at a good clip. When they reached the truck, Stella sat in the backseat and Jack settled the fawn into her arms.

Papa Pete sat up front with Rufus in his lap.

He let out an enormous sigh as soon as Jack turned the truck onto the road.

"What's wrong?" Jack asked. From his tone, Stella could tell he was smiling.

Papa Pete's tone couldn't have been more different. "Going to all this fuss for a *fawn* is a waste of time." The way he said *fawn* made it sound like an insult. "Come next fall, that critter will be shot anyway. Less trouble to die now."

Stella looked down at the bundle on her lap. Most of the fawn was still covered with her shirt. But she could feel the small creature trembling. The fawn didn't like being in the backseat of a truck. She belonged in the woods with her mother.

Stella couldn't hold her tongue any longer. "Maybe fawns would live longer if people like you stopped hunting," she said.

"Stella," Jack said in a warning tone.

"Well, I just don't understand why people hunt," Stella insisted.

"And I don't understand why I should have to explain myself to my own granddaughter," Papa Pete said tensely.

Nobody spoke for the rest of the ride into town. Stella was ready to get away from her grandfather. She was relieved when her father pulled up in front of the clinic.

Jack rushed inside to get Anya.

Moments later they came hurrying out. Anya poked her head into the truck. "Pete," she said.

"How are you, Anya?"

"Just fine. Okay, Stella, I'm going to take her now." Anya opened the back door. She lifted up the long-legged fawn and started toward the clinic with her.

Stella slipped off the seat and began following her aunt.

"Stella!" Jack called. "I'm going to take Papa Pete home. Then I'll be right back to get you."

"Okay!" Stella called impatiently. She wanted to get inside and find out what was happening with the fawn.

"Stella!" Jack called.

She spun around. "Yes?"

"Say good-bye to your grandfather."

"Bye, Papa Pete," Stella said sullenly. Then she turned and quickly trotted after Anya.

"Nice splint," Anya said as she slid the trembling fawn down onto an exam table.

"Thanks." Stella felt a rush of pleasure. She wanted to be a veterinarian more than anything in the world. Anya's praise made her feel great.

"Here, hold on to her while I get cleaned up."

Stella grabbed the fawn with both hands. "It's okay," she murmured quietly. "Nobody is going to hurt you anymore."

The tension Stella had felt in the truck was starting to fade. Spending time with Anya always made her happy.

Anya turned away from the sink where she was scrubbing her hands. She gave Stella a big, pleased smile. "Hey—it's good to see you! How have you been?"

"Fine," Stella said, feeling almost shy. She'd seen her aunt only a few times in the past two weeks. "You look tired," she added.

"I am." Spring was a busy time for Anya.

Ranching was a big business in Montana. All over the countryside cows were giving birth. Some needed help during their labor. Once in a while, nursing made the mother cows sick. And even if they were healthy, the thousands of newborn calves needed all sorts of shots. Some of the ranchers had asked Anya to help dehorn the calves and attach their ID tags.

Anya's pretty eyes were ringed with dark circles. Her short coppery hair looked windblown and wild. Stella knew her aunt had been working sixteen-hour days.

But Anya had never stopped to wonder if she had the energy to help the fawn. Stella felt a surge of love for her aunt. She wanted to be like Anya when she grew up—*not* like Papa Pete.

Anya finished putting on her surgical gear and gathering her supplies. She came back to the table and gave the fawn a shot of medicine to put her to sleep. The needle prick startled the fawn. She struggled to get away, but Anya and Stella both held on tightly.

"Let's hold her until that takes effect," Anya said.

"Sure." Stella stared down at the fawn's light brown fur for a long moment. "Aunt Anya?"

"Hmm?"

"Where did you learn to be a vet?"

"School. Montana University. And then Tufts for Veterinary School—that's in Massachusetts—back east where the pilgrims landed." Anya laughed as if she were remembering something pleasant.

"How long did it take?"

"Oh, a while. Four years of college, then four years of vet school. Eight years. A long time."

"But it was worth it," Stella said.

Anya glanced up and gave Stella a wink. "I think she's asleep."

Stella watched as Anya shaved a patch of fur off one of the fawn's front legs. Anya inserted a needle into a vein and attached a bag of intravenous solution.

Then she went to work on the injured hind leg, snipping away pieces of torn fur. "So . . . is she going to be okay?" Stella asked.

"Well, the good news is that her leg isn't broken," Anya said. "I'll clean up this wound, and then I'll want to keep an eye on her for a few days. But we'd better figure out what to do with her after that. She'll need someone to be her mom until she's old enough to survive in the woods alone."

"How about me?" Stella forced herself not to think about the fawn's real mother. Did the doe wonder what had happened to her baby?

Anya laughed. "Actually, I was hoping for someone *furrier*. The fawn is going to need feeding every three hours. You can't do that and go to school at the same time. But I read that goats will sometimes adopt fawns and nurse them."

"Oh." Stella couldn't help but sound disappointed.

Anya gave her a sympathetic look. "We don't want her to spend too much time with humans.

That could lead to disaster after we release her. She'd be expecting hugs from hunters."

"Papa Pete said helping her was stupid," Stella said bitterly. "He said someone will probably just shoot her anyway."

"Well, I figure she deserves a chance at life," Anya said. "Same as the rest of us."

Stella nodded. "So we need to find someone with a goat to adopt her?"

"That's what I was thinking."

"How about the Capras?" Marisa Capra was one of Stella's friends from school. She loved animals—maybe even a little *too* much. Marisa baby-talked to her cat and put hair ribbons on her horse. She even made a birthday cake for her favorite pig!

"Free lodging at Belle's Bed and Breakfast?" Anya made an I-should-be-so-lucky face. "She'd be one fortunate fawn."

Belle's Bed and Breakfast was the Capras' little hotel. Tourists flocked to their plush rooms, mountain views, and whirlpool baths. The Capras also had a working farm—but it was mostly to amuse their guests. Norma sometimes joked that the Capras' pig pen was cleaner than her own house. They had a couple of beautiful horses, a 700-pound pig, and three of the most spoiled dairy goats in Gateway.

Stella heard a knock at the door. She turned around in time to see Jack poke his head into the exam room. "How's it going?" he asked.

"Not bad," Anya said. "The fawn's going to be just fine."

"Great!" Jack said. "So are you ready to go, Stella? School tomorrow. And didn't you tell me you had an oral report to give?"

"But . . ."

"Go on home," Anya said without looking up. "Everything is under control here."

"Okay," Stella agreed reluctantly. "But I'll come by tomorrow to help feed the fawn. And I'll ask Marisa if they'll adopt her."

"See you tomorrow." Anya sounded distracted.

At home, Stella found her mother in the sunroom. She was doing a load of laundry. "A four-year-old from Albuquerque got raspberry ice cream all over my uniform," she told Stella.

"Yuck!" Stella said. Then she gave her mother a kiss on the cheek.

Tourists from all over the world visited Goldenrock. The crowds were biggest during warm weather. From May to September, Norma spent lots of her time at work giving tours. She told the visitors about the plants and animals that lived in the park.

"So how was mushroom hunting?" Norma

tossed a couple of her dark green uniforms into the machine. "Did you have fun with Papa Pete?"

Stella felt her smile fade as she thought about the mountain lion. "Mom—we saw a lion."

"Fantastic!" Norma's face lit up, and Stella saw envy in her mother's eyes. She knew Norma had seen a mountain lion only once—even though she spent hours in the woods each week. The big cats like to stay hidden.

"Not so fantastic," Stella said with a frown. "Her face was full of porcupine quills."

Now Norma's smile faded, too. She banged the washing machine lid closed and pushed the start button. She headed for the kitchen, and Stella followed. Jack was at the sink, washing mushrooms.

"I was thinking we could track the lion and help her . . ." Stella held her breath—unsure of how her mother would respond. Norma's time was precious during the summer. She got only one day a week off work.

Norma considered the idea as she inspected the mushrooms Jack was laying out on the counter. "Muffin, I'm not really the best person for that job. Mountain lions have proven very talented at staying away from me."

"But, Mom, we have to do *something*," Stella

wailed. "We can't just sit around and let the lion starve."

"I agree," Norma said. "But I think we need an expert's help."

"Like who?" Stella asked.

"How about Papa Pete?"

"No!" Stella stomped her foot. Then she sent a guilty look toward her father. She took a deep breath and tried to calm down. "Papa Pete knows about the lion. And he didn't offer to help her."

Jack looked thoughtful as he scooped the mushrooms onto his cutting board. "Dad seems to think that giving medical care to wildlife is a waste of time."

Norma frowned and then gave Stella a brief nod. "Okay, let's hike in on my next day off. Saturday."

"Great!" Stella hugged her mom around the waist. She wished they didn't have to wait two days to help the lion, but at least now she felt certain the lion would survive.

"Someone is hungry." Jack pointed at Rufus with his elbow. The little dog was sitting at Jack's feet, patiently waiting for a scrap of food to drop.

"I'll take care of him," Stella said.

Stella fixed Rufus's dinner. He was still eating when Stella's older sister, Cora, came home from her job at the stables. The family worked together to finish dinner. While they ate, Jack and Stella told Cora and Norma all about their eventful afternoon in the woods.

By the time the dishes were done and Stella sat down to do her homework, it was almost seven o'clock. Rufus napped on her lap while she put a few last touches on her oral report. The assignment was for science class. They had to choose a species of animal and describe where it lived.

The big kitchen clock read 9:10 by the time Stella finished. Yawning broadly, she closed her books and then gently shook Rufus awake. He rose wearily to his feet and licked Stella's mouth.

Stella carried the little dog across the room. She knelt down and put him in his kennel. The sturdy plastic kennel was meant to be his own safe spot in the house. A comfy cushion Norma had bought lined the bottom. And Rufus had a nylon bone inside to chew on.

Rufus lay down in the kennel. But the moment Stella flipped off the kitchen lights, he bounded out. He jumped up, putting one tiny paw on Stella's calf. He looked at her with pleading eyes.

"Aw." Stella scooped the dog into her arms. "Don't look so sad, Rufus. The kennel isn't that bad."

But she didn't really understand why Rufus had to sleep downstairs. Keeping him in the kitchen made sense before he was house trained. But now that he'd learned to do his business outside, making him sleep downstairs seemed kind of mean.

Stella worried that he got lonely by himself. After all, he was only twelve weeks old. But Norma and Jack had laid down the law. So Stella carried the puppy back toward the kennel, feeling awful.

Rufus let out a low, sad whine.

That was enough for Stella. "Okay, Rufus," she whispered. "You can sleep in my room tonight. Just be quiet so Mom and Dad don't find out."

On the playground before school on Friday, Stella told Marisa about the fawn. Josie Russell, Stella's best friend, listened quietly.

The story made Marisa's dark eyes fill with sympathy. "I'll ask my mom if we can help the fawn," she promised. "But—I don't understand how Daisy could nurse her. She doesn't have any babies of her own."

"You mean she doesn't have any *kids* of her own," Josie put in. She lived on a big ranch, and even though her family didn't raise any goats, she knew a lot about farm animals.

Marisa giggled. "Kids. Right."

"Does your mom milk the goat?" Josie asked.

"Sure." Marisa made a face. "She makes goat cheese with the milk. Yuck."

"So the goat is producing milk every day." Josie sounded a tiny bit impatient. Stella knew Josie thought Marisa was too mushy about animals. "That means she can nurse the fawn. But your mom won't get as much milk for cheese."

"Oh, I'm sure she won't care about that," Marisa said.

Josie rolled her eyes. The Russells' ranch was a business. Josie's daddy had to make money on their livestock. He would never help a wild animal if it meant losing money. Stella was glad the Capras didn't feel that way. The fawn needed *someone* to help.

"Give me a call as soon as you know," she told Marisa when the bell began to ring.

"I will," Marisa said solemnly.

The girls went inside. School got underway and passed swiftly, falling into the rhythm of routine. Mrs. Jaffe, the girls' teacher, didn't get around to the science reports until late in the afternoon. She called on Stella about ten minutes before the end of school.

"Good luck," Josie whispered.

"Thanks," Stella said under her breath. She picked up her notes and walked to the front of the classroom. Her heart was galloping away in her chest. Giving oral reports usually didn't

bother her, but she'd picked a topic that often made people mad.

Stella faced the class and took a deep breath. "My animal is the wolf," she announced. "And I'm going to talk about how they used to live in Montana."

She paused—noticing that some kids sat up straighter or looked at their friends. Only one kid in the class wasn't paying attention. Jared Frye—who sat way back by the iguana cage—was staring at Harley.

Harley was the class iguana. He'd been in the classroom only a week. Before that, he'd belonged to the school janitor, Bob. When Bob decided to move to Alaska, he asked Mrs. Jaffe if she would adopt Harley. Mrs. Jaffe agreed and brought in a small aquarium for the iguana.

But when Bob came to drop off Harley, the iguana was bigger than the aquarium! He was more than two feet long. Bob installed a large wooden and wire cage for Harley in the back of the classroom. Inside was a big branch for the iguana to climb. A light hanging above the cage helped keep him warm.

Mrs. Jaffe seemed scared of Harley. But Jared was fascinated by him. Mrs. Jaffe put Jared in charge of feeding Harley, and Jared checked all the reptile care books out of the library. Seeing Jared stare into Harley's cage was nothing out of the ordinary. What *was* strange was his expression. He looked worried.

"Stella?" Mrs. Jaffe said.

"Oh—right!" Stella glanced down at her first note card and began her report. "For centuries, gray wolves prowled the forest of what is now Montana. They had few enemies until European settlers arrived here in the early 1800s. People were scared of the wolves because they had big teeth. Wolves sometimes killed farmers' animals.

People worried that they might attack humans, too."

"Hey—just like the Big Bad Wolf!" Duncan Crowe called out. He was a dark-haired kid with big glasses. He *always* had something to say.

"Wolves don't really eat people," Stella said quickly. "People only *thought* that. The Big Bad Wolf is just a character in a story."

"Watch out, I'm a wolf!" Duncan turned and growled at Henry Percy, who sat next to him.

"That's enough," Mrs. Jaffe said. "Go on, Stella."

Stella glanced down at her note cards again. "People were scared of the wolves. So they shot and poisoned them. At one time, the government paid hunters a reward for each wolf they killed. By the early 1930s, no wolves were left in Montana."

"None?" Mrs. Jaffe asked.

"Well . . . maybe *one* would wander down from Canada once in a while," Stella said. "But one or two wolves isn't enough to keep the animal populations in balance. See . . . the wolves used to hunt coyotes. Now that we don't have any wolves, the forest is full of coyotes. That makes life harder for the foxes and badgers because the coyotes gobble up all the rodents they like to eat. Many, many other kinds of animals have been affected, too. That's why the program to return the wolves to Goldenrock is so important."

"That's what you think," Henry Percy mumbled under his breath. Stella heard him only because he was sitting in the first row.

Henry's comment didn't surprise Stella. She knew lots of people didn't want the wolves returned to the woods. Deer hunters worried that the wolves would kill all the deer and ruin their fun. Ranchers were still worried about their farm animals. Henry's dad was a cattleman, like Josie's.

But Stella's family had been fighting for the return of the wolves since back before she was born. Norma was one of the scientists in charge of returning the wolves safely.

Mrs. Jaffe gave Stella a nod. "Does anyone have a question for Stella?"

Marisa raised her hand. "What happened to the wolves we saw?" A few weeks earlier, Stella's class had gone on a field trip to the park. They saw eight wolves arrive in the back of a horse trailer. The wolves had been caught in Canada. Eventually they would be let loose in Goldenrock.

Stella smiled. "Oh! Well, those wolves are living together in a big pen."

"Why doesn't your mom let them out?" Marisa asked.

"The wolves have to get used to each other first," Stella said. "And they have to get used to Goldenrock, too. It takes a while."

Stella looked up. Jared had his nose practically pressed up against the wire of the iguana cage. What was he looking at?

"Any other questions?" Mrs. Jaffe asked.

"I don't understand how eight wolves could make any difference in such a big forest," Amanda Foster said. She was a smart and serious girl.

"Well, there aren't going to be just eight," Stella explained. "Six more wolves arrived in the park last week."

"More?" Henry spoke louder this time.

Mrs. Jaffe held up a finger, and Henry slumped down in his chair.

"Yes," Stella said with excitement. "One of the new wolves is a big, black male called Seven. My mom thinks he's an alpha!"

"What's an alpha?" Mrs. Jaffe asked.

"Oh . . ." Stella paused to think. That wasn't an easy question to answer. "See, wolves live in extended families. Scientists call them packs. The top male and female in a pack are called the alpha male and alpha female. They're usually the only wolves who mate."

"I see," Mrs. Jaffe said. "Did Seven's wolf wife come along, too?"

"No," Stella said. "When my mom and the other scientists caught the wolves, they tried to capture complete packs. But the first group had this female—she's called Six—who seemed like an alpha. Her mate was never found."

"Poor Six," Marisa said with a pout.

Stella grinned at her. "The scientists were pretty sad, too," she said. "They want to release at least three alpha couples. That's the only way we're going to get enough baby wolves to grow a healthy population. The first two couples arrived in the first group of wolves. Six and her mate were supposed to be the third couple."

"So now what?" Marisa asked. "Are they going to search for her mate some more?"

Stella shook her head. "They're going to try a blind date! They're planning to put Six and Seven together in a pen."

"Woo, woo!" Duncan made his eyebrows dance around.

Everyone ignored him.

"You've got to understand something," Stella said in a low, secret-telling voice. "Putting two wild wolves who are *strangers* together in a pen is totally risky. Two things can happen. They might make friends. Or they might kill each other."

Marisa gasped—just like Stella had known she would. She was about to explain that the scientists would keep a careful watch on the wolves. But before she could say a word, Jared jumped to his feet.

"Mrs. Jaffe," he yelled. "I think Harley is dead!"

• 5 •

For a moment, nobody moved. Then the kids jumped up and ran back to Harley's cage.

Stella dropped her note cards on Mrs. Jaffe's desk. She joined the others, pushing to get to the front of the crowd.

The dismissal bell rang, but nobody left.

"Man, it didn't take us long to kill him," Henry said.

"What did you do to him, Jared?" Duncan asked in a teasing voice.

Jared didn't laugh. "I didn't do anything," he said tensely.

Stella was scanning the cage, but she didn't see the iguana. Harley spent most of his time up high on his branch. He liked to get as close as possible to the lightbulb that hung over his cage.

"Where is he?" Stella whispered.

Josie pointed down low. Stella finally spotted Harley. He was in a corner of the cage, lying on his scaly back. His feet were up in the air. He looked dead, all right.

"Okay, kids," Mrs. Jaffe said in a businesslike tone. "It's time for everyone to head home. I'll take care of Harley."

Josie made a face. She backed away from the cage. So did most of the other kids. But Jared stayed close to the wire, peering in.

"Clem's picking me up," Josie told Stella. "I'd better go."

Stella nodded. Clem was Josie's sixteen-year-old brother. He often picked her up for the long ride back to their ranch.

"I think I saw him move," Jared announced.

Stella had been planning to leave with Josie and Marisa, but now she let her friends go ahead. She watched the iguana carefully. Nothing happened. Still, Stella thought it was best to be certain.

"Mrs. Jaffe," Stella said. "I think we should make sure he's dead."

The teacher looked doubtful. But Jared quickly

nodded. "Let's poke him and see if he moves," he suggested.

Stella opened the cage door and reached her hand back into the corner. She held her breath as she gently touched Harley's side.

Harley feebly wiggled his long green fingers.

"Did you see that?" Jared demanded.

"He's alive!" Stella exclaimed. "I've got to take him to my aunt's animal clinic right away. Maybe she can save him!"

"But . . ." Mrs. Jaffe seemed confused.

"All I need is a box to carry him in," Stella said. "I can take him on my bike."

Mrs. Jaffe snapped out of her daze. "I'll look in the supply closet."

"Thanks," Stella said.

Mrs. Jaffe banged around in the closet for a few minutes. Then she emerged, carrying a good-sized cardboard box. She stood back as Stella again reached into Harley's cage and gently lifted him out. Stella put the iguana into the box. She packed some newspaper around him so he wouldn't slide around during the trip.

Stella picked up the box and started walking out of the classroom.

"Do you need some help?" Mrs. Jaffe asked. "Do you want a ride?"

"No, thanks," Stella said. Traffic was always

heavy just after school let out. She could get to the clinic faster on her bike. "I'll tell you what happens on Monday."

Jared trotted along beside Stella. He held open the door that led to the parking lot. "I'm coming with you," he announced.

Stella was surprised, but she didn't protest. Jared had been in her class only about a month, and she never paid much attention to him.

Outside, Stella realized that the big box wouldn't fit on her bike. The basket in front was too small. She was thinking about walking when Jared pushed up an old red one-speed.

"I can put that on my rack," he offered.

Stella firmly attached the box to Jared's bike. They rode into town, pedaling as hard as they could. *Harley is alive*, Stella thought. *But just barely*. She didn't want him to die because they hadn't gotten him to the clinic fast enough.

Please let Anya be here, Stella thought as she pedaled up to the clinic. She showed Jared where to park his bike, and then led the way up the three back stairs. The door was open. Jared carried Harley's box into one of the examination rooms, and put it down on a stainless steel table.

"Anya!" Stella bellowed.

A moment later, Anya came charging down the

stairs that led to her apartment. Her basset
hound, Boris, was right on her heels.

"What's up?" Anya asked—ready for action.

"Sick iguana."

"Where did you get an iguana?" Anya asked.

"School," Stella said. "His name is Harley."

"Would you put Boris in my office?" Anya was
already hurrying toward the examination room.

"Sure," Stella said. She clapped one hand

against her thigh, and started toward Anya's office. "Come on, Boris."

Boris followed Stella, his long ears swaying as he trotted along on his stocky legs. In the office, he flopped down on his bed. Anya trained him to stay there while she was treating animals in the clinic.

Stella waited until Boris was settled. Then she hurried into the exam room. Anya had already lifted Harley out of his box. He lay motionless on the table. His eyes looked as if they had sunk into his skull.

Jared was standing against one wall. "This is Jared," Stella told Anya. "He's in my class at school."

"Hi, Jared," Anya said. But she was looking at Harley. She gently touched the iguana and watched his weak response.

"What do you think is wrong with him?" Jared asked.

"Hard to say." Anya had stepped away from the table. She was sliding a slender needle into a syringe. "Any idea what he's been eating?"

Jared looked nervous. "Well, the books I got out of the library said iguanas like to eat a bunch of different stuff. I've been feeding him all kinds of green leaves—spinach, collard greens, and dandelions. I mix them up in the blender at home and bring the mixture to school in my lunch box."

"You do?" This was news to Stella.

Jared nodded solemnly.

"Sounds like you've been doing a good job."

"Oh—but not for long," Jared said. "We just got Harley from Bob, the janitor."

"Well, then, it's possible that Bob was giving Harley too much protein." Anya's tone was distracted. She was drawing a tiny amount of blood into the syringe. "This is strange," she murmured.

"What?" Jared demanded.

"Harley's blood is . . . Jell-O," Anya said.

Stella and Jared exchanged looks. "Jell-O?" Stella asked.

Anya laughed a little. "I mean that it's very thick. It's barely flowing into the syringe. Pumping this stuff must be forcing his heart into overdrive."

"Why is his blood so thick?" Stella asked.

"I'm guessing kidney failure," Anya said. "Maybe caused by an infection. We'll know more after I run some blood tests."

"Can you save him?" Jared asked.

"Well, I'm sure going to try," Anya said. "The first thing we need to do is thin out that blood. Some saline solution should do the trick."

Anya quickly weighed and measured Harley. She did some calculations on the back of an envelope. Finally, she inserted a needle into one of Harley's veins and attached a small bag of saline solution.

Jared tapped Stella on the arm. "What is that stuff?" He cast a suspicious look at the saline.

Stella laughed. "Oh—it's just salt water."

Jared still looked worried, so Stella added, "Doctors give it to people all the time."

"Are you sure it won't hurt him?" Jared asked.

Stella smiled. "I'm positive!"

Jared pulled a chair up to the exam table. He gently ran a finger over one of Harley's front legs. "Don't worry," he said softly. "I'm not going anywhere."

Anya caught Stella's eye and gave her a wink. "You have a great bedside manner," she told Jared.

Jared just shrugged.

While they waited for the solution to drip into Harley's bloodstream, Anya headed toward the laboratory with the blood sample. Stella followed along. She used the phone in the lab to call home and tell her dad where she was.

"How's the fawn?" Stella asked when she got off the phone.

"Go out back and see," Anya suggested. "Her

surgery went well and I've given her seven feed-ings so far. I got her bottle-trained after about the third."

"Want me to feed her this afternoon?" Stella offered.

"Do I ever," Anya said. "I think I got about two hours of sleep last night."

"It's Friday," Stella said. "I could sleep over and do the feedings tonight."

Anya smiled. "If it's okay with your parents, that would be a big help. Let me show you what I've been doing."

The fawn was getting eight ounces of goat milk in a bottle. Anya showed Stella how to fill the bottle, fasten on the nipple, and warm it in the microwave.

Anya and Stella went to the fawn's pen to-gether. She was on her feet, watching them ap-proach. Her oversized ears perked up when Stella's shoes squeaked on the floor.

"You go ahead," Anya said quietly. "Let's see how she likes you."

Moving quietly, Stella let herself into the pen. She held the bottle at arm's length. The fawn came forward slowly, her small black nose twitching like a rabbit's. She grabbed the nipple and began to suck.

"That wasn't so hard," Stella said quietly.

Anya groaned. "You should have been here for her first feedings. I had to sit on her and sneak the nipple into her mouth. She fought hard until she tasted the milk. Then—bingo! She decided she was more hungry than scared and started to drink." Anya sounded pleased by her success.

The fawn's soft brown eyes were locked on Stella's. Stella could see the fawn's delicate throat working, and could count the tiny ribs under her coat.

"She's so beautiful," Stella whispered.

"I know," Anya said. "Just remember that she'll be safer if we keep her wild."

Stella nodded. "I won't forget."

Anya went back to the lab to run the tests on Harley's blood. For the next ten minutes, Stella stood as quietly as possible. When the fawn finished her bottle, Stella resisted an urge to pet her. Instead, she backed out of the pen.

In the exam room, Anya was just removing the needle from Harley's vein.

"Stella, you've got to see this." Jared sounded excited. "Harley is, like, totally better!"

"Not *totally* better," Anya said with a smile. "But he is much more animated."

Stella got closer and examined the iguana. He immediately whipped around and fixed one eye on her.

"He's going to live?" Stella asked.

Anya nodded. "He needs more fluids and some medication to clear up that infection. But, with proper care, he could live another eighteen years."

Jared beamed at Stella. "You saved his life!"

"I think you did," Stella said, with a laugh. "You were the one who noticed Harley was sick."

Jared ran a finger over the iguana's head. "Well, I guess Harley is lucky we were both there. Mrs. Jaffe was ready to toss him."

Stella frowned thoughtfully. "I don't think Mrs. Jaffe likes Harley much."

"She definitely doesn't."

"That's interesting," Anya added. "Because I don't think the classroom is a good home for Harley."

"Why not?" Jared demanded.

"Well, Harley probably finds being around so many people stressful," Anya said. "Also, iguanas can spread salmonella—a type of bacteria that lives in reptiles' stomachs. Salmonella can make people very sick. Especially kids."

Jared's shoulders drooped. "But if someone else adopts Harley, I'll never get to see him."

Anya put a hand on Jared's shoulder. "Why don't *you* take him home? I'll teach you how to care for him so you're not exposed to salmonella."

"My dad would never let me." Jared sounded very sad as he petted Harley. "He doesn't think I'm responsible enough to have a cat. And an iguana is lots more work."

"True," Anya said thoughtfully.

"But you've been helping Mrs. Jaffe take care of Harley," Stella said. "Maybe you should tell your dad that."

Jared shrugged. "I'll ask. But I'm sure he'll say no."

Stella and Jared helped Anya set up a place for Harley in the boarder's room.

The cage itself was no problem. Anya had a wood and wire cage in a quiet corner. Over the years, it had housed a trumpeter swan with a broken beak, a pet rabbit with an infected toe, and a piglet with pneumonia. Stella added a water dish and a tree branch, and it was ready to go.

But finding the proper lights and getting them adjusted took some time. Iguanas are cold-blooded, which means their bodies don't create any heat. Instead, they absorb heat from their environment. Harley needed the lights to stay warm.

Marisa called just as Jared was heading out the door. "I tried you at home," she told Stella excitedly. "Your dad told me where you were and said it was okay to call. How's Harley?"

Stella laughed, still feeling surprised by the iguana's recovery. "Much better. Did you talk to your mom?"

"Yes! And she loves the idea of helping the fawn. When can you drop her off? And can Anya show us what to do?"

Five minutes later the arrangements were made. Stella and Anya would drop the fawn off the next afternoon.

By the time Stella left the clinic, it was almost dinnertime. She rode her bike home as fast as possible.

Rufus greeted her at the door. He shook his tail so hard that his entire body swayed. He put his head down low and then jumped up, barking with excitement.

Stella knelt down next to him. "Hello, boy! I'm happy to see you, too."

"I already walked him," Cora called from the couch.

"Thanks," Stella said. "Did he eat?"

"Not yet."

Stella could smell their own dinner bubbling away in the oven. Cora always cooked dinner on

Friday nights. Sometimes her cooking was fabulous. Sometimes it wasn't. At least whatever this was, it smelled good.

"Is Dad here?"

"In the office."

Stella went in and said hello to her dad. He gave her permission to spend the night at the clinic. Stella wandered back into the kitchen, picked up the phone, and punched in Josie's number.

Rufus stood at her feet, gazing up with longing in his eyes. "Okay, I'm about to feed you," Stella promised him as she listened to the phone ring.

"Yup?"

Stella made a face. Clem had answered the phone. Josie's older brother was *not* Stella's favorite person. Like his father, he was against the wolf reintroduction, and he even tried to break up a pro-wolf rally Cora and Stella had organized.

"May I please speak to Josie?" Stella said stiffly.

"Yup." Stella heard Clem drop the phone with a clank.

"Thanks," Stella muttered.

Rufus was still giving her that hungry-dog look.

Stella tucked the receiver between her shoulder and ear. She picked up Rufus's bowl and set it on the counter. She opened a cabinet, pulled out the bag of puppy kibble, and scooped half a cup into Rufus's bowl.

"Here you go, boy!" She put the bowl down in front of Rufus.

Rufus's tail twitched. He sniffed at the food. Then he backed away from the bowl and lay down with his front paws stretched straight out. He sighed and rested his chin on his paws.

Stella frowned. "What's the matter, boy? Aren't you going to eat?"

Rufus gave her a mournful look without moving.

Stella thought for a moment. Her mother insisted that dry food was best for Rufus. But that was assuming he *ate* it. Missing dinner couldn't be good for a growing puppy. And Rufus obviously had no intention of eating the dry food.

She opened the cabinet again and pulled out a

tiny can of dog food. When she popped open the top, Rufus jumped up. He wagged his tail and licked his lips.

Stella scooped the moist food into a small dish. She put it into the microwave and warmed it slightly. She added the warm food into Rufus's bowl. This time, the little dog dug in with vigor.

"That's better," Stella said with a smile.

"Hello?"

"Oh—Josie! Where were you? I've been waiting forever."

"Sorry. I was out in the barn. Guess what?"

"What?"

"Esmeralda's udders are filling!" Esmeralda—or Esme—was the Russells' favorite mare. She was a beautiful chestnut quarter horse with a kind face and an uncanny intelligence. Esme was eleven months pregnant. The fact that her udders were filling with milk meant that the foal would be born soon.

"That's great!"

"Yup! Dad says she'll deliver in about four days. Oh Stella . . . I can't *wait* until the foal gets here."

"I know. Raising it is going to be so much fun."

"Except . . ." Josie took a deep breath. When she spoke again, her voice was much lower. "My dad is worried. I can tell because he's acting like a big grumpy bear. I'm scared for Esme. If something happened to her . . ."

"Don't worry," Stella said. "We'll take good care of her. I'll make sure Anya knows she's about to deliver. Hey—you could tell Anya yourself. I was calling to see if you wanted to spend the night at the clinic."

"Hmm . . . only if I can get home early tomorrow. Dad says Esme needs a special place to deliver. I'm going to scrub out one of the empty stalls and get it ready."

"I'll help," Stella offered. "We can do it tomorrow morning."

"Okay," Josie agreed eagerly.

Norma came in while Stella and Josie were deciding what time to meet at the clinic. By the time Stella got off the phone her entire family was milling around the kitchen. She had just enough time before dinner to wash her hands and set the table.

"So did Six and Seven meet today?" Stella asked as soon as the family sat down together.

"Oh, yes." Norma had a secret little smile, which made Stella think nothing bad had happened.

"Well . . . let's hear it!" Jack demanded.

Norma put down her fork. "We released Seven into the pen this morning. He trotted right over to Six and sniffed her all over. Then he . . ." She paused for dramatic effect.

"Bit her?" Stella guessed.

Norma shook her head. "He laid his head across the back of her neck."

"Is that good?" Cora asked.

"Yes and no," Norma said. "In wolf language, it means I like you—but I also outrank you."

"How did Six like that?" Jack asked.

"Not a bit!" Norma seemed amused. "She stiffened, snarled, and scooted away."

"Cold," Cora said.

Norma nodded. "It was chilly in that pen for *hours* while those two growled at each other. But they gave us some hints they just might like each other."

"Like what?" Stella asked.

"Well . . . every few minutes they touched noses and sniffed some more. Then they went right back to the snarling routine. But they weren't fooling anybody. We could tell they liked each other. By the time I left work today, they were pacing around the pen in perfect step and grooming each other."

"So they're, like, married now?" Jack asked.

"They're a couple," Norma said.

Cora rolled her eyes. "This reminds me of a play we're reading at school."

Jack looked interested. "What play?"

"*Romeo and Juliet.*"

"That's a movie," Stella said. "Everyone dies in the end."

"Yeah," Cora agreed. "But it's so romantic."

Jack chuckled. "So when are Romeo and Juliet going to be released?"

"Next week," Norma said with a smile. "Same time as the rest of them."

"This is perfect," Stella said. "Now you're going to be able to release three alpha couples just like you planned."

Norma nodded. "I still can't believe it," she said with a faraway look in her eyes. "After all this time, the release is actually going to happen."

Stella looked out the kitchen window. It was twilight, and the woods that ran up to her backyard were in deep shadow. She shivered, realizing that in just a few days' time these woods would be changed forever. Soon Stella would look out her window and know it was possible that wolves were hidden in the twilight shadows.

The world was about to become a little more wild.

Stella welcomed the change. She liked the idea of the animals gaining back some of the land that humans had stolen from them over the years. They deserved it.

7

Anya dropped Stella and Josie off at the Russells' around 9:30 on Saturday morning. She was heading out to the Rosebud ranch on some routine calls, but she promised to come back for Stella around noon so that they could deliver the fawn to Marisa.

The girls walked toward the horse barn along a split log fence that enclosed what the Russells called "the near corral"—about ten acres of hilly pasture land.

Josie kept yawning. Stella felt a bit bleary-eyed, too. She and Josie had fed the fawn every three hours throughout the night. The fawn had been dozing peacefully when they left the clinic. Stella had felt like curling up next to her in the straw.

"Here comes Esme," Josie said with a smile.

As the horse started toward them, Stella could see that her sides were bulging out slightly. But she trotted up to the fence at a good pace and nickered hello. Josie reached through the wooden rails and rubbed her neck.

"She looks good," Stella said.

Josie nodded happily.

"Where are the other horses?" Stella asked. The Russells kept six—but she saw only four in the corral.

Josie looked up and did a quick survey. "Bess and Babe are gone. Dad and Clem must be out riding fence."

The Russells owned a thousand head of cattle, and they all worked hard to keep the ranch going. Repairing the miles of fence that kept the cattle on the property was one job that always needed doing.

"Come on," Josie said. "Let's do our work first. We can take a ride when we're finished."

"Sure," Stella agreed.

Josie led the way up to the stables. The building was like the rest of the Russell ranch— functional, but not fancy. The barn walls were made of cement block, the floors were concrete, and the boxes had sliding metal doors.

"This is the box we're going to move her into."

Josie stopped at an empty box that was a bit larger than the others.

"Looks comfy," Stella said.

"It will be," Josie said. "But it needs a good cleaning." The girls went down to the tack room, which was tucked away at one end of the barn. Tack is the name for horse-related gear. The small space was crammed full of saddles, saddle blankets, saddle soap, buckets, pitchforks, brooms, sponges, combs, and hoof picks.

Josie filled two buckets with water and disinfectant. Then she found a couple of oversized scrub brushes and carried everything back to the box.

The girls scrubbed every inch of the walls, floor—even the manger which would hold Esme's hay. They pulled the hose into the stall and washed everything down well. Then they spread an extra thick layer of straw and sawdust on the floor.

By 11:00, when they were finished, Stella was hot, tired, and sweaty. Sawdust was up her nose. Bits of straw stuck to her T-shirt and socks. But seeing the big smile on Josie's face made her forget all that.

"Everything is ready," Josie said proudly. "Come on—let's go for our ride now. I have to exercise Esme anyway."

"Really?" Stella asked. "Doesn't she need to rest?"

"Nope. Dad wants me to exercise her right up until the day she foals. I don't work her too hard. Come on. You haven't been riding in ages."

Josie didn't have to press the issue. Stella loved to ride.

The girls went down to the corral and collected Esme and Honey—a white mare who was almost as old as Stella. They saddled up back in the barn. The sun was high overhead as Josie led their way out into the pasture behind the Russells' house, setting a gentle pace.

Stella had ridden Honey dozens of times, and she felt comfortable on her. The meadow was speckled with dandelion blooms and a hawk was circling high overhead. A few clouds were massing over the distant mountains, and a chilly breeze was blowing off the snow-covered peaks.

Once the horses were warmed up, the girls nudged them into a trot. At the tree line, Josie turned back to the barn. Halfway there, she let Esme slow down to a walk. Stella sat up straighter, gave Honey her head, and prodded her gently with her knees. Honey broke into a canter—thundering past Josie and Esme.

Stella was out of breath by the time they reached the barn. She slowed Honey to a walk

and took her around the ring a few times to cool her down.

"That was fun," Stella said when Josie rode up. "Thanks."

"No problem," Josie said. "Old Honey needs some exercise."

The girls were unsaddling the horses when Anya's truck pulled into the yard.

Anya got out. "How's Esme?" she called to Josie.

"Fine, I think."

Anya came over and gave Esme a quick exam. "She looks great. And I'd almost guarantee that she's going to deliver in the next few days."

Stella smiled at Josie. "I guess that means you don't want to go mountain lion hunting later this afternoon."

"I better not," Josie said. "I want to stay close to Esme."

"Okay . . ." Stella said reluctantly. "But call me as soon as anything happens!"

"Promise," Josie said.

Stella and Anya went over to the truck and climbed inside. The fawn was already loaded into the back. Anya had pulled a burlap sack over the fawn, allowing just her head to stick out. The fawn stared wide-eyed at Stella all during the short drive to the Capras'.

Marisa and Mrs. Capra were waiting for them on their porch. Anya parked next to a car with a California license plate. She lifted the fawn out.

Marisa gasped. "She's so pretty! She looks just like Bambi!"

Stella laughed and shook her head. She could imagine how Josie would react to that comment. "Yeah," she said. "Except for one thing—she's not a cartoon!"

"We cleaned out a stall for her." Mrs. Capra led the way into the tidy, fresh-smelling barn. The fawn had a nice box stall all to herself.

Anya put the fawn down in the straw and loosened the burlap bag. The fawn quickly scrambled to her feet. She gave Anya an indignant bleat which made everyone laugh.

"I think she's hungry," Anya said. "Why don't we see how Daisy does?"

"She's just in the next stall," Mrs. Capra said.

Daisy turned out to be a beautiful white and black goat, with a wide head and muzzle. She had a deep chest and strong straight legs. As they approached her box, Daisy came up and nuzzled Marisa's hand. She had a sweet face.

Only one thing worried Stella. Daisy didn't have any ears. The skin around the ear canal was wrinkled, but that was it.

"What happened to her ears?"

Anya laughed. "She's a LaMancha. Their ears always look that way!"

"Can they hear okay?"

"Sure."

"Oh." Stella could feel her face heat up.

She was relieved when Anya and Mrs. Capra began bustling around in the goat's box. They tied Daisy up snugly and gave her a pan of grain.

As soon as Daisy was busy with her snack, Anya carried the fawn in. The animals gave each other a long wary look, and then they both looked away. Daisy kept eating while the fawn hobbled up to Anya and nuzzled her hand.

"She's looking for her bottle," Stella said.

Anya sighed. "Belle, would you mind holding Daisy? I think we need to give the fawn some lessons."

"Sure." Mrs. Capra moved into the box. She knelt down and wrapped her arms around Daisy's neck.

"Perfect," Anya murmured. She picked up the fawn and carried her over to Daisy. She pushed on Daisy's rump so that the goat sat and spread her legs. Gently, she pushed the fawn's face down onto the goat's udder.

The fawn didn't need any more encouragement. She grabbed on to one of Daisy's nipples and began to suck.

Daisy drew back—looking surprised for a moment. Then she remembered the grain and went back to eating.

"Aw," Mrs. Capra and Marisa said at the same time.

Anya winked at Stella. The Capras were mushy all right!

"Please remember not to turn the fawn into a pet," Anya said to Belle and Marisa. "Trusting humans too much could be dangerous for her."

Belle nodded solemnly. "I made a sign for our guests." She came out of the stall and showed them a beautifully painted sign. In color letters on a white background, it read, THIS FAWN IS WILD, AND WE WANT TO KEEP HER THAT WAY! PLEASE KEEP YOUR DISTANCE.

Anya smiled. "That's great!"

After everything was settled in the barn, Mrs. Capra asked Stella and Anya inside for lunch. Stella had some terrific tomato soup, asparagus salad, and a homemade muffin. By the time she finished eating, she could hardly hold her head up.

After getting up to feed the fawn in the middle of the night and working so hard on Esme's stall, Stella was pooped. Luckily, Anya got her home in time to take a quick catnap before the lion hunt.

Norma and Stella left the house just after four o'clock.

"I picked up my rifle from work," Norma said as Stella climbed into the front seat.

Stella had heard about the rifle. It worked with compressed air and had a telescopic sight. Instead of a bullet, it shot a dart syringe full of medicine that would make the lion sleep. For now, the weapon was packed up in its case.

They stopped by the clinic. Anya stowed a backpack full of surgical instruments in the flatbed. She'd assembled everything they'd need to remove the quills from the lion's tongue, mouth, and lips.

"Thanks," Norma said.

"Good luck!" Anya called as they drove away.

Norma parked in the lot at the trail head. There was only one other truck there—and its owners were leaning against the bumper, changing out of their hiking boots.

"Late start for a hike," the man called as Norma and Stella headed for the trail with their gear.

"Maybe," Norma said to Stella. "But this is the perfect time to catch a mountain lion. They're most active in the evening."

Stella felt a surge of hope. She was certain her mother would be able to track the lion down and save its life. Stella led the way up the trail. After about twenty minutes, she reached the clearing where she had seen the lion with Papa Pete.

"This is the place," Stella whispered.

Norma nodded, looking around. "It's the perfect kill site for a lion." She pointed to the woods. "That heavy undergrowth gives her a good place to hide."

Stella let out all her breath. "So what do we do now?"

Norma popped open the rifle case and began assembling it. "We wait and hope your friend shows up. If she does, I want you to stay close by me. Mountain lions sometimes attack humans—especially little kids."

"I'm not little," Stella protested.

"I know. But let's play it safe."

Stella nodded. She watched her mother finish preparing the rifle. Then she found a stump to sit on. She waited quietly, and carefully scanned the edge of the woods.

Norma chose a spot nearby. She sat cross-legged with the rifle resting on her knees.

Before long, Stella was bored. She longed to talk to her mother—but she was afraid the lion would hear her voice and stay away.

The minutes slowly ticked by.

Stella found herself growing sleepy. She

wished she could stretch out on the grass. But what if she missed the lion while she was napping? She fought to stay awake, even though her head felt so heavy that she had to rest it on her palms.

Suddenly, Stella startled and woke up—not knowing for a second where she was. Then she remembered and looked over to see her mother still sitting in the same position.

"How long have we been here?" Stella whispered.

"Twenty minutes," Norma said.

"That's all?"

Norma nodded. "You should have brought a book."

"I wish I had."

After a while, Stella grew used to the waiting. Sitting in the woods doing nothing was almost like being on a long car trip or fishing. She daydreamed while keeping half an eye out for the lion.

Slowly the light in the forest began to fade.

Norma sighed and stood up. She groaned as she stretched her stiff muscles. "I'm afraid we're going to have to admit defeat."

"But we've been here for hours," Stella wailed. "I don't understand why we didn't see the lion."

"Actually, it's not so surprising," Norma said.

"You said Papa Pete thought the lion was just passing through. And even if she was a resident, female mountain lions often have territories that are more than forty miles square. She could be on the other side of the county by now."

"So why did you agree to come out here?"

Norma frowned and exhaled loudly. "Well, I thought those porcupine quills may have slowed her. I thought she might be too weak from hunger to go far."

"Then we shouldn't give up," Stella said.

"Well, muffin, we can't do any more today," Norma said. "Even if the lion appeared, I can't see to aim the rifle. And the next time I have off is a week from now."

"So we'll come back then."

Norma put a hand on Stella's shoulder. "There's not much point. By then some other animal will have killed her, or she will have died of starvation."

Stella sighed deeply. She knew her mother was just being practical. But she couldn't give up now.

• 8 •

Stella felt sad and frustrated the entire way back down the trail. She had been so certain her mother could help. Now she felt hopeless.

Norma drove into town and stopped at the clinic to drop off Anya's equipment. Anya was in her office when they came in. Boris was stretched out at her feet. He banged his tail against the floor and half-raised his head in greeting.

"You lazy dog," Stella said affectionately. She knelt down to pet Boris's head.

"Any luck?" Anya asked. She'd changed out of her work clothes and into a pair of clean sweats.

"Nope." Norma leaned against the doorway and yawned.

"Are you going to try again next week?"

"It will be too late by then."

Anya took a look at Stella and reached out to smooth her hair down. "Hey—don't look so bummed out."

"I just don't want the lion to die."

"Me neither." Anya sighed. "I wouldn't mind a break from the grind around here. Spending some time in the woods sounds good to me."

"You'll help the lion?" Stella threw her arms around her aunt. "When can you go? How about tomorrow?"

Anya laughed. "Wait a second. I was going to say that the only problem is that I have no idea how to track a lion."

"That's exactly what was wrong with today," Norma said. "We just sat around hoping the lion would find *us*."

"That's better than doing nothing," Stella insisted.

"Not much," Anya said. "Maybe we should ask Papa Pete for help. He knows the woods like nobody else. And since it's not hunting season, he has plenty of free time."

Stella groaned impatiently. She didn't understand why Norma and Anya wanted Papa Pete's help. They knew as well as she did that he was a hunter. How could she trust him?

"I already told Mom—he's not interested in helping the lion."

Anya reached out a foot and rubbed Boris's ear with her big toe. "Pete may not care much about the lion. But I bet he'd love to spend the afternoon with his granddaughter."

"Wrong! All we ever do is fight."

"That's because you're so much alike," Norma said.

"Are not!"

Norma winked at her. "You sounded just like Papa Pete when you said that."

"Mom!"

"Listen, Stella, it's your choice," Anya said. "But if you really want to help the lion, you should call Papa Pete."

"He'll say no."

Norma smiled and shook her head. "You don't know that."

"I'll show you." Stella asked her mother for Papa Pete's number, then picked up Anya's phone and punched it in. Someone scooped the phone up on the first ring.

"Sullivan's Back Country Guides. Pete speaking."

"Papa Pete. Hi. It's Stella."

"Oh. Stella. Hello." Papa Pete sounded surprised, and Stella realized this was the first time she had ever called him on the phone.

"Anya and I want to find that lion," Stella said

uncertainly. "She—um, we wanted to know if you would help us."

"She's gonna remove them quills, eh?"

"Yes," Stella said tensely. She braced herself for a long lecture about wasting her time on lost causes or fighting the laws of nature.

"What time you thinking of going?" Papa Pete asked gruffly.

"Um—" Stella raised her eyebrows at Anya. "Sometime in the late afternoon tomorrow? We figured she'll be easier to catch then."

"We'll start first thing in the morning," Pete said. "Dogs can get a better scent before it gets too hot. We'll meet at the trail head at seven-thirty."

"Wait a second," Stella said. "I don't know if Anya can—"

But the phone had gone dead.

"He wants to meet tomorrow morning at seven-thirty," Stella said.

Anya shrugged. "Works for me."

"I can drop you off on my way to work," Norma said.

"Fine," Stella said with a sigh.

Papa Pete was already at the trail head when Norma and Stella arrived in the driving rain the next morning. Stella was surprised to see that he had brought three dogs with him. She recognized only one—old Maxie.

"When did Papa Pete get those puppies?" Stella asked.

Norma shrugged. "Beats me." She parked the truck and climbed out to say hello to Pete.

Stella got out, said a quick hello, and immediately went to where the dogs were tied to Papa Pete's back bumper.

Maxie was a gentle black and tan coonhound. His hazel eyes were intelligent, and he whimpered happily as Stella scratched behind his long ears. She knew that Papa Pete had trained Maxie to hunt lions—but she had no idea how that worked.

The two puppies looked as if they were from the same litter. Stella judged them to be about a year old. They were big, muscular dogs with wide chests and large heads. Their coats were short, dense, and a reddish-brown color. They were excited, watching Papa Pete, straining at their leashes, anxious to get into the woods.

Stella looked up as Anya pulled into the parking lot. "Hey—I see you've brought your two new beauties," Anya called to Pete as she hopped out of her truck.

"Yup. Thought I'd see what they could do."

Stella was surprised. When had Anya met the

pups? But then she guessed what had happened. Anya must have given the pups their shots—because when they saw her, they sat back on their haunches and moaned. Dogs often had bad memories associated with Anya.

Norma came back to Stella. "Try to stay dry," she said, pulling the hood of Stella's raincoat more snugly around her head.

"I'll try."

"See you this afternoon," Norma said. "And good luck."

Papa Pete approached the pups with a short strap. He snapped one end around each of their collars.

"Why are you doing that?" Stella demanded.

"So they'll run together," Papa Pete said. "Supposed to stop one of them from chasing off after a deer or rabbit. Doubt it will work, though."

"What are their names?" Stella asked.

"Ace and Caliber."

Anya came up and let the pups give her a good sniff. "Rhodesian Ridgebacks," she told Stella. "Great hunting dogs. Aren't they beautiful?"

"Yes," Stella whispered.

"Maxie's got only a few more good years in him," Papa Pete said. "I'm a'hoping one of these here dogs will take his place."

Stella felt miserable. Papa Pete did have beautiful dogs. But he kept them for only one reason. So that they could help him kill lions and other wild animals.

"Well—best get started." Papa Pete gathered up all three leashes and led the way into the woods. Stella was carrying a backpack with the surgery supplies. Anya had a bag with the air rifle and darts.

Hiking through the woods was soggy business. The trail was muddy, and droplets of water dripped off the cottonwood trees. Stella was thankful for her long sleeves and sturdy jeans.

When they reached the clearing, Papa Pete led Maxie to the exact spot they had first seen the lion. He unhooked Maxie's leash. The dog trotted along the line of trees with his muzzle right up against the ground. His tail wagged intensely and he let out a few excited baying barks.

"Here, hold these dogs," Papa Pete told Anya. He held out Ace's and Caliber's leashes, which Anya took.

Papa Pete began walking along with his head down. He was more or less following Maxie.

"Stella, why don't you help out?" Anya suggested.

"Doing what?" Stella asked.

"Looking for tracks," Anya said.

Stella shrugged. Maxie had disappeared into

the underbrush, and Stella did her best to follow, getting soaked in the process. Almost immediately, she began seeing tracks in the mud. But she wasn't sure if they were Maxie's—or the lion's.

She examined one perfect print for several minutes. There were five indentations in the ground. One was large and shaped almost like an upside down heart. The other impressions were shaped like teardrops and evenly spaced.

To Stella, the print looked just like one of Maxie's. But she wanted to be sure. She called Papa Pete to check it out. He crashed through the underbrush without any hesitation. Anya stayed in the clearing, holding on to Ace and Caliber.

"Nice print."

"Is it a lion's?"

"Most definitely."

"How do you know?"

Papa Pete picked up a stick, which he used as a pointer. "The prints are clean. Not smudged. That tells me that the animal that made them was *walking*."

"So?"

"So haven't you ever noticed how a dog walks? They're impatient—trotting over there, trotting back. Dog prints are messy. Cat prints are neater. Also, look close."

Stella knelt down nearer to the ground.

"See that little slit in the mud?"

"Mmm hmm."

"That's where the lion used her claws to get more traction."

"How do we know it's *our* lion?"

"Won't know that until we catch her. *If* we catch her."

Papa Pete raised his voice. "Here Maxie!"

Seconds later, Maxie nosed her way into the underbrush.

Papa Pete pointed at the print. "Here it is," Papa Pete said in an excited tone. "Here, here, here!"

Maxie dropped her nose into the print, inhaled deeply, and gave one happy staccato bark. The dog was quivering with excitement. She gave Papa Pete a look full of longing.

"Go git 'em, boy!" Papa Pete said.

Maxie burst into motion, quickly disappearing into the dense weeds.

"Let the pups go!" Papa Pete called to Anya.

A moment later, the pups pushed past Stella and followed Maxie into the woods.

Stella backed out of the underbrush after Papa Pete.

"Found the track," Papa Pete told Anya. "But following the dogs is going to be hard work."

"Well, let's get moving," Anya said. "We don't want them to get too far ahead."

Papa Pete led the way up the trail, moving at a good clip. Stella came next. Then Anya.

Somewhere off to the left they could hear the shrill sound of Ace and Caliber barking. After about five minutes, the trail steepened and they began to gain elevation. The rain coming down now was only a fine mist. Occasionally, Stella would get a view through the trees of the valley opening up below them.

They climbed for about twenty minutes before the underbrush thinned out. Papa Pete veered off the trail, heading straight toward the dogs' distant barking.

Stella was hot and tired and wet. Hiking off the trail was hard work. The leaves underfoot were slick from the rain, and she slipped several times. Twigs that Papa Pete pushed aside snapped in her face. Still, she forced herself to keep up. She didn't want to give Papa Pete any reason to call off the hunt.

The dogs' barking was slightly louder now. But

Stella didn't see how they would ever catch up with them. They were moving too fast.

Suddenly, Papa Pete stopped. He held up a hand without turning around.

"What is it?" Anya whispered.

"Hear Maxie?"

The dog was barking steadily, making more noise than Stella knew he could make. Stella heard Ace and Caliber join in.

"They got 'im," Papa Pete announced.

Stella's heart began to thud with excitement. She felt a burst of energy.

It took them another ten minutes to climb down into a gully, cross a small stream, and scramble up the other side. The dogs never stopped barking.

Suddenly Stella saw the mountain lion. She had climbed a dead lodgepole pine and was standing on a limb twelve feet up. From below she was all big paws and oversized shoulders. She wasn't snarling the way a frightened house cat might. Instead, she seemed curious, yawning, then lowering her head and trying to get a better look at the action on the ground.

Stella could see the porcupine quills sticking out of her face like thick whiskers. The big cat looked skinny—her ribs and spine were visible under her fur.

Papa Pete grabbed the dogs, hooked on their leashes, and handed them to Stella.

Maxie sat at her feet with a sigh, licking his chops. Ace and Caliber flopped down, stood up, circled, and settled down again.

Papa Pete took off his backpack. He pulled out a bottle of water and a pie tin. He poured some water for the dogs, who lapped it up. Papa Pete took out a tarp and unfolded it. "We're going to hold this under that cat and catch her when she falls," he announced.

"Okay," Stella said solemnly.

Anya knelt down and began assembling the air rifle. "What do you think she weighs, Pete? Eighty pounds?"

" 'bout that."

Anya opened a plastic case and drew some anesthetic into a dart syringe. She opened the bolt and loaded the dart.

"I've never fired one of these," Anya admitted. "Would you mind, Pete?"

Papa Pete came and took the rifle. "It's okay to take the tarp, Stella. The dogs will stay put."

Stella dropped the dogs' leashes. They didn't move.

Anya picked up one side of the tarp. Stella lifted the other and pulled it taut. She kept her eyes on the lion, frightened of somehow missing her.

Pete settled the rifle onto his shoulder and peered through the eyepiece. A dart left the rifle with a *thwock*. It hit one of the lion's hind legs and dangled there.

The lion cringed, which made Stella cringe. She expected the lion to fall immediately, but the cat only shifted her weight and continued to stare down at them. The dart was hanging from her skin.

"Okay, Stella. I'll take over." Papa Pete took Stella's side of the tarp and motioned for her to step back.

Five minutes passed before the lion's head began to sag. She yawned widely and stretched out on the limb, hugging it with her front paws.

Papa Pete stood gazing up at her. "Looks mighty comfortable. Hope I don't have to go up there and pry her loose."

Anya and Stella exchanged nervous looks. Stella was surprisingly glad that Papa Pete was there. Who else would have known to bring a tarp? Or been prepared to climb up after the lion?

Suddenly, the lion's hind legs slipped out from under her.

"Watch it," Papa Pete told Anya.

The lion was swinging from the tree limb, holding on with her front paws. She tried to hook one hind leg back up, but she was too sleepy to make it happen. In slow motion, the lion's front paws loosened.

"Here she comes!" Stella called.

The lion plummeted down. Anya and Papa Pete grunted as she hit the tarp. They supported her weight and lowered her gently to the ground.

Anya knelt down and ran one hand over the lion's flank. "What a beauty. Well, I don't think she's going to need any more drugs. She's pretty limp."

Papa Pete picked up the dogs' leashes and backed them out of the way.

Stella crept forward as Anya pried open the lion's mouth and examined her tongue. "Yow. No wonder this lady is so skinny." The lion's tongue was swollen and angry-looking.

Anya opened a medical kit and pulled out tweezers, scalpels, and scissors. She set to work, carefully removing dozens of quills from the lion's face, tongue, gums, and throat. She injected some vitamins and antibiotics.

Stella spent the next hour at her aunt's side. She was filled with wonder, amazed at this opportunity to sit so close to a lion and examine every inch. She had a beautiful silvery-tan coat and incredibly huge paws. The lion's broad nose was covered with little nicks—maybe from her fight with the porcupine. Occasionally her muscles twitched, which reminded Stella that this creature was alive—and would be dangerous awake.

Papa Pete stayed nearby, too. The dogs waited patiently—apparently enjoying the rest.

When Anya finally finished, she and Papa Pete carried the cat a little way into the woods. The lion lifted her head with a grunt a few times, but then slumped back down. Her tail, her ears, her nose twitched.

"She's beginning to wake up," Anya said quietly. "Let's go."

Stella paused to take one last look at the lion.

Papa Pete was looking, too. "Maybe I'll see you this winter," he told the cat.

Stella frowned with distaste. She certainly hoped Papa Pete wouldn't see the lion during hunting season. But if Papa Pete hadn't hunted—if he hadn't trained Maxie to track lions—this lion would have died.

She knew Papa Pete thought all their efforts that day were a waste of time. And she was pretty sure he had come out only because of her. The thought made her feel strange. She'd always assumed Papa Pete didn't like her much.

Anya led the way back toward the trail, humming softly to herself. Papa Pete and the dogs went next. Stella followed him, staring at the back of his head and wondering how she could thank him for helping save the lion.

They reached the trail and started down. Now there was room to walk together, and Stella fell into step with Papa Pete.

Stella took a deep breath. "Well, we actually caught her."

"Yup."

"Maxie was amazing."

Papa Pete looked at her with raised eyebrows.

"Earlier . . . when we first found the track? I couldn't believe the way she waited until you said it was okay to follow it."

Papa Pete's expression hardened. "Rufus could be just as well-mannered. That dog is bad, but he's not stupid."

Stella's first reaction was a flash of anger. Why did Papa Pete have to be so mean about Rufus? He wasn't *bad*. He was just a puppy. But as they continued to walk, her attention was drawn to Ace and Caliber. They were puppies, too. Their behavior was nowhere near as controlled as Maxie's. But, on the other hand, they were angels compared to Rufus.

"Did Ace and Caliber go to obedience school?" Stella asked.

"I trained them myself."

"How?"

Papa Pete looked at her—as if deciding whether she really wanted to know. "You've spent a lot of time studying wolves," he said.

"Yeah?" Stella was confused.

"Well, wolves and dogs are closely related. Dogs are pack animals. Training them, you've got to prove you're the alpha in the pack. Rufus thinks he's the alpha."

Stella gave her grandfather a doubtful look. But he didn't seem to notice.

"If you want Rufus to be a good dog, you must act like a good master. An alpha. Take charge. Give Rufus treats only when he earns them by obeying your orders. Feed him only at mealtimes. Make him sleep in his kennel."

Stella shot Papa Pete a surprised look. How did he know she let Rufus sleep in her bed?

"Training Rufus will make him a happier dog," Papa Pete said.

Stella disagreed—so she didn't say anything. Being strict might be a good idea if you're raising a hunting dog. But she didn't see any reason to be mean to Rufus.

For the rest of the hike out, Stella stayed quiet. She still felt thankful to Papa Pete. But it seemed as if they would never agree about anything important.

When they got back to the trail head, Anya and Papa Pete chatted for a few minutes. Then Stella climbed into Anya's truck for the ride home.

"Bye, Papa Pete," Stella said out the window. "Thanks for helping us."

Papa Pete had already turned toward his truck. He simply raised a hand in reply.

Back at home, Stella found Jack working at the computer. He had a magazine article due the next day and was reading it aloud. Stella told him all about the lion hunt, and he said Rufus had been cooped up inside all day.

"I'll take him for a walk," Stella said. As soon as she pulled the leash out of the closet, Rufus began to jump up and bark with excitement.

"I can't hear myself think!" Jack called.

"We're going!" Stella opened the front door and let Rufus out. He ran onto the porch and then turned to wait for her. Stella pulled the door shut. She knelt down to clip on Rufus's leash.

The little dog's body stiffened. He jerked his head toward the street, suddenly alert to . . . something. Stella followed his gaze for a moment, but didn't spot anything.

"What's the matter, boy?"

Stella looked down and began turning his collar around so the hook was facing her. She was just about to clip on the leash when Rufus lurched forward. He bounded down the steps in one fluid motion and charged across the grass.

"Rufus!" Stella yelled sharply. "Come back!"

The little dog streaked across the yard. He sprinted across the sidewalk.

Stella jumped to her feet. "Rufus—No!"

Rufus ran into the road.

Stella saw a little red car barreling straight for him. She covered her eyes when the car's brakes began to squeal.

● **10** ●

"Ruf! Ruf, ruf, ruf!"

Rufus was still alive. But was he hurt? Stella slowly lowered her hands from her face. She opened her eyes just in time to see Rufus tear into the yard across the street. The red car had stopped in the middle of the street. Now Stella recognized it as Mrs. Barber's Volkswagen.

"Sorry about that!" Stella called to Mrs. Barber, who had pulled into her driveway.

Mrs. Barber waved. "Just missed him!"

Stella felt shaky as she dashed across the street.

"Rufus, come here!" she called.

The little dog continued to bark at something under one of Mr. Synder's box elders.

Stella snuck up from behind and snapped Rufus's leash onto his collar. Then she bent down to see what he was nudging with his nose.

"Ohh . . ." Stella breathed. It was a baby bird! The bird had a pale gray head. His white chest was spotted with black marks, and he had a patch of orange feathers on each breast. A baby robin.

Rufus again nudged the bird, which played dead.

"No!" Stella pushed Rufus aside with her foot and gently picked up the robin. She could feel the bird's tiny heart pounding. He cocked his head and looked at her with one inky eye.

Stella carefully ran her fingers over the bird's legs, which were barely as thick as spaghetti. She examined his wings, which seemed undamaged.

She looked up in the tree. No nest. Stella thought for a moment. Somewhere, sometime she had read a book or an article that said robins teach their babies how to catch worms. Naturally, they have to do this on the ground. What if Rufus had interrupted this little bird's lesson? And scared away his parents?

Stella gently placed the bird on the ground. She scooped up Rufus and carried the struggling, protesting puppy back to the house.

She went next door to the Barbers', explained about the baby bird, and asked Mrs. Barber to keep her dogs and cat inside. None of the other nearby neighbors had animals that they let loose.

Stella borrowed her dad's binoculars. She sat on the front porch and guarded the baby bird from a distance. The little bird already seemed less afraid. It hopped two or three times. Stella was hoping the bird's mom or dad would come back now that Rufus was out of the way.

While Stella watched the bird, she thought about how close Rufus had come to getting hit. She thought about all the injured dogs that came into the clinic. Usually, the dogs were hurt because of something their owner had done. They let the dogs run loose. Or let them ride in the flatbed of their pickup truck.

Stella always felt sorry for the heartbroken owners. But she blamed them a little, too. She thought that if they had been more responsible, their dogs never would have gotten hurt.

Now she realized she had been too quick to judge. She'd almost let Rufus get hit by a car. If he had been better trained, he would have come when she called him, and not—

Stella gasped. Another bird had come into view! A big orange-breasted robin hopped right up to the baby bird. This had to be Mom or Dad robin. The baby bird was going to be okay. Stella lowered the binoculars, feeling relieved.

Walking back inside, she made a decision—Papa Pete was right. She had to start showing Rufus she was boss. Having a disobedient dog was just too dangerous—for Rufus, and for the people and animals around him.

Stella called Josie just before dinner.

"Esme still hasn't delivered," Josie reported when she came to the phone. She sounded tired and frustrated. "Dad said not to worry. But I *was* worrying, so he let me call Anya."

"What did she say?"

"She said not to worry! First foals are sometimes a month late. That means we might be out of school before Esme ever delivers!"

Stella laughed. "I doubt that will happen."

"It better not!" Josie said.

That night, Stella put a wiggling Rufus to bed in his kennel. She lay awake in her own bed and listened to him whimper. His pitiful whining made her chest ache. A thousand times, she thought of going downstairs and rescuing him.

But Stella forced herself to be strong. This is for his own good, she told herself. She thought about how well-behaved Papa Pete's puppies were. And she made herself remember the awful moment when she'd thought Mrs. Barber had hit Rufus.

After almost half an hour, Rufus finally quieted down.

Stella felt sad and worried as she drifted off. And she was nervous as she came downstairs the next morning. She was afraid Rufus would be mad at her for making him sleep alone in the kitchen.

But Rufus greeted her with a happy bark. Relieved, Stella scooped him up and gave him a hug. She felt a surge of hope. Training him might not be impossible after all! Maybe I'll call Papa Pete after school and tell him, Stella thought.

She ate breakfast and then climbed on her bike. The ride to school was perfect—the sky was bright blue and the air felt warm.

Stella found Marisa on the playground. "How are things going with the fawn?" she asked.

"Great!" Marisa's eyes were sparkling. "Daisy is letting the fawn nurse without even being tied up. Our hotel guests love watching them! But we make them keep their distance."

While the girls were talking, Duncan and Henry ran up.

"How's Harley?" Duncan demanded.

"Oh!" Stella had forgotten that some of her classmates didn't know Harley was still alive. The weekend had been so busy! "He's much better," she said. "But my aunt doesn't think he should come back to school."

"Because we almost killed him?" Duncan asked.

"It wasn't our fault that Harley got sick," Stella said. "There was something wrong with his kidneys."

Jared joined the group. "Anya thinks school is too noisy for Harley."

"Maybe Stella's mom can feed him to the wolves!" Duncan was the only one who laughed at his joke.

Jared nudged Duncan with his shoulder. "Hey—be quiet! Harley is my pet now. Watch what you say about him."

Stella stared at Jared. "What about your dad?" she asked.

"Anya called him," Jared said with a happy smile. "She told Dad I was already doing a great job taking care of Harley." He stood up straighter and raised his chin, looking proud.

Stella patted Jared on the back. "That's great!"

"Dad wouldn't agree at first. But Anya said we could bring Harley back to the clinic if things don't work out."

"You won't have to do that," Stella said confidently.

The bell rang. The kids began to file inside.

"Where's Josie?" Marisa asked.

"She's late again," Stella said with a shrug.

Josie was late to school about once a week. Clem and Josie each had a long list of chores to do before school. Sometimes they were delayed because a cow escaped or one of the horses was sick.

Class started. An hour passed, and then two. Josie still hadn't shown up. Stella started to get excited.

"I bet Esme is delivering her foal!" she told Marisa at lunch. "I'm going over there right after school to see what's happening."

The afternoon dragged on and on. They had a spelling test. Then more kids gave their science reports. Jared's species was the Giant Green Iguana. Stella did her best to pay attention, but she was wild with impatience.

Finally, the last bell rang. Stella hurried out of the building, grabbed her bike, and headed toward the Russell ranch.

The ride helped calm her impatience. She quickly pedaled through the afternoon traffic in downtown Gateway and followed Route 2A out of town. Just past the turnoff for her house, the road began to climb. The hill forced Stella up out of her seat. She pushed the pedals with all her might.

Pastures on either side of the road were brilliant with yellow balsamroot blossoms. Bees buzzed from flower to flower. The temperature was much warmer than Stella was used to. Her T-shirt was sticking to her back by the time she turned into the Russells' drive.

Stella rode her bike right up to the stable. She leaned it against the wall and went inside. "Josie?"

Josie stuck her head out of the box they had prepared on Saturday. "Hey . . ." she said softly.

"Hey! Is anything wrong? You seem upset."

"Just tired. All of my horse books say mares deliver at night. They also say emergencies come up quickly. So I slept out here last night."

Judging from Josie's rumpled clothes and the straw in her hair, she hadn't been inside all day.

Stella looked into the box. "Wow," she murmured—surprised by the change that had come over the horse.

Esme seemed restless. She tossed her head, nickered, and pawed at the ground. Her eyes were wild; her flanks were wet with sweat. The Russells had wrapped her tail in white bandages, but she still twitched it back and forth. As the girls watched, she bent her front legs and lowered herself onto the ground.

"Is it okay for her to lie down?" Stella whis-

pered. Horses spend most of their time on their feet. And she wasn't sure if lying down could somehow hurt the foal.

Josie nodded quickly. "She's been doing that for hours. Daddy says it's normal."

Esme turned her head back to bite at her flanks. Then, with a powerful shift of her weight, she was up on her feet again. More tail twitching, another toss of her head, and she lay back down.

Josie sighed.

"Did you eat any lunch?" Stella asked.

Josie shook her head. "Daddy's been out in the

pastures all day, and I didn't want to leave Esme alone."

"I'll make you a sandwich," Stella offered.

"Thanks."

Stella went inside. She rustled up a tuna salad sandwich, poured a glass of milk, and found an apple that was only slightly bruised. She was carrying everything back to the stables when she heard Josie yell.

"Something's happening!"

Stella broke into a run. The apple bounced off the plate, but she didn't stop to pick it up.

• 11 •

When Stella got to the box, Josie grabbed her arm with one hand and pointed to Esme with the other.

A white membrane was pushing out from under Esme's tail. The horse seemed calmer now. She lay down and blinked languidly.

"It's okay," Stella said. "I think the foal is finally coming. Are you supposed to call your dad?"

"Yes." Josie sounded a little shaky.

Like most of the ranchers Stella knew, Mr. Russell carried a portable phone with him when he rode out to check on his cattle or fences. Josie could call him and tell him what was happening. Stella hoped he hadn't ridden out to a remote pasture. If he had, it might be half an hour or more before he got back to the ranch.

"Go on and call him," Stella said.

Josie ran toward the house.

Stella began to speak soothingly to Esme. "Good girl. You're doing a fine job."

Esme strained, the muscles in her neck tightening as she fought some internal battle.

"That's it," Stella murmured. She hoped Esme couldn't tell that she'd never seen a foal delivered before. Anya was rarely called in to help, because most horses gave birth easily.

Esme strained again, and two of the foal's legs appeared. Stella caught her breath as two shiny hooves came into view. The damp matted coat looked dark.

Stella's chest ached with happiness. This was it. Esme was finally giving birth.

And Josie was missing it. . . .

"Get back here, Josie," Stella whispered. She didn't want her friend to miss the foal's arrival after waiting so long.

Josie jogged back into the stables just as Esme was straining again. "Dad's about ten minutes away. He said the forelegs should appear first and we should call back if we can see only one . . ."

She gasped and covered her mouth when she saw the foal's legs. Even though Stella couldn't see Josie's mouth, she could tell from her eyes that she was grinning.

Esme strained again and again. Josie hid her face each time the horse had a contraction. But Stella watched to make sure the foal and Esme were both all right.

Another contraction came—and the head of the foal appeared.

"Look, look!" Stella whispered to Josie.

The foal stared back at them. Its dark eyes were already open and alert. The dark hair on its head was clumped and almost curly. It was holding its ears back.

Esme turned around and had a look, too. She rested for what seemed like a long time. Then she strained again, and the rest of the foal swiftly appeared.

"Is it a boy?" asked Stella, peering into the stall.

"Yes," Josie said proudly. "A fine colt." Both Esme and the colt lay quiet, breathing and resting.

"What do we do now?" Stella whispered.

"Daddy said not to do *anything*," Josie told her.

The girls heard the sound of horses' hooves pounding up outside. A moment later, Mr. Russell came striding into the barn.

He wore boots and dark blue jeans held up

with a belt sporting a big silver buckle. The sleeves on his denim shirt were neatly buttoned. He had a beat-up cowboy hat on his head and a red bandanna knotted around his throat.

Mr. Russell came up and laid a hand on Josie's shoulder. As he looked in on Esme, a big smile brightened his tanned, lined face. "Why, would you look at that? A big fine colt."

Josie smiled up at her father.

Esme struggled to her feet. Stella gasped as the thick, white umbilical cord broke.

Mr. Russell patted Josie's back. "Go on down to the tack room and grab the bottle of iodine so that we can clean up the colt's umbilical cord. I keep a little jar next to it. Bring that along, too, and any towels you can find."

"I'll help," Stella offered.

When the girls got back, Josie handed the supplies to her dad. Iodine is a type of disinfectant. Norma sometimes used it on Stella's scrapes and scratches.

Mr. Russell uncapped the iodine and poured it into the wide-mouthed jar. "Mares can be protective of their foals. But you've been hanging out in the stable so much lately, Esme probably thinks you're related."

Josie smiled uncertainly.

"Dip the colt's stump into the iodine," Mr. Russell told her. "Make sure you do a good job now. We don't want that little fella getting sick."

Josie's hands were shaking as she took the jar. But she marched into the box, knelt down next to the colt, and positioned the jar so that his stump got a good covering of iodine.

"Mmm hmm. That looks good. Now dry him off." Mr. Russell tossed Josie some towels. She rubbed the colt down until he lost his shiny look.

As Josie came out of the box, the colt started to struggle to stand. He got his front legs under him first, and then clumsily rose onto all fours. His legs seemed to be made out of rubber. But he quickly gained confidence—and stability.

Esme began licking the colt with her large tongue, almost knocking him over in the process. He struggled away from her, nosing under her belly until he found her udder.

"Everything looks perfect here," Mr. Russell said with satisfaction. He went outside to take care of the horse he had been riding.

Stella leaned against Josie.

Josie gave her a sideways hug.

The girls stood together for a long time, silently taking in the cozy scene. By the time they left the barn, the sun was low on the horizon.

"I'd better start dinner," Josie said. "Did you ask your folks if you could stay?"

Stella gasped. "Nobody knows where I am!" she exclaimed. "I was going to call home once I got here—but I forgot."

Josie shook her head. "I'm sure your parents will understand. Come in and give them a call."

Stella called home. No answer. "I hope someone walked Rufus," she said guiltily. She hung up and tried her mother's cellular phone.

"Hello?"

Stella felt a little happy pang that came from hearing her mother's voice. "Mom! Hi. Where is everyone?"

"Hmm. Spread all over the county. Jack's got that conference in Billings, remember?"

"I guess." Stella vaguely recalled her father signing up for some sort of meeting about writing.

"Cora is with me," Norma continued. "And you're at Josie's, right?"

"How did you know?"

"I called Anya's looking for you. She said Esme was delivering her colt. I put two and two together and called over there about twenty minutes ago. Josie's dad told me you two were out in the stable ogling the new arrival. I didn't want to interrupt you."

"Thanks Mom. He's a real beauty. Listen—did someone take care of Rufus?"

"He's been fed, walked, and cuddled." Norma didn't sound angry that Stella had let the rest of the family take care of Rufus. In fact, she sounded in very good spirits.

Stella giggled. "So where are you going?"

"To work."

"But it's after six o'clock!"

"I know. I'm working late."

"Well, I guess I could have dinner here."

Josie nodded vigorously.

"If that's what you want. Or I could pick you up and take you into work with me." For some reason, Norma sounded amused.

"Why?"

"I thought you might want to see the wolves released."

"Tonight?" *That* explained Norma's good cheer.

"In about half an hour."

"Pick me up!" Stella said.

Josie gave Stella a puzzled smile as she hung up the phone. "You aren't staying?"

"No. Thanks for the offer, though. Josie, I'm going with Mom to release the wolves!"

Stella couldn't wipe the smile off her face, and she bounced up and down like a little kid. She'd waited for this moment for so long. But she never thought that she'd actually *witness* it. She wondered if her mother had somehow planned it so she and Cora could go along.

Josie gave her a quick, bitter smile. "Great."

Stella hated the way this issue kept coming between her and Josie. She gave Josie a quick hug, pretending that a distance hadn't opened up between them. "I'll see you tomorrow at school, okay?"

"Okay." Josie kept her eyes on the hamburger meat she was forming into patties.

Stella let herself out into the cool backyard. The sky was just beginning to turn a beautiful orange. She went back to the barn, collected her bike, and coasted down the driveway to the road.

Norma drove up a few minutes later.

Cora got out to help Stella lift her bike into the flatbed. "Tell me about the colt," she said excitedly.

She kept up a constant flow of questions. Stella told her sister everything about Esme's delivery—which didn't give her much time to think about the wolves.

Ten minutes later, Norma pulled over to the side of the road. A couple of green park service trucks were already parked there.

Four adults were standing around talking. Stella knew Mack, one of her mother's co-workers. He was talking to another man in a park service uniform. Stella also recognized Nina Leland, a reporter from the *Idaho Falls Times,* who had interviewed her and Cora during their pro-wolf rally. A man wearing a khaki vest was a photographer from the paper.

Norma gave Cora and Stella each a flashlight, although it wasn't dark enough to need them yet. The group started into the woods. Nina quizzed Mack as they all carefully made their way up the shadowy path. But the entire group grew quiet when they reached the pen where the pack had lived for the past six weeks.

"Look at them go," Nina whispered to no one in particular.

"Don't like people much," Mack responded.

The wolves had fled to the far reaches of the pen. Most were pacing nervously back and forth.

"Which one is Juliet?" Cora whispered.

"There." Norma pointed to a big wolf near the far line of the fence. She was shying away from them, with her head low. She looked almost coy as she glanced in their direction. She was beautiful, solid black, powerful-looking.

"And there's Romeo," Norma added. "Isn't he magnificent?"

He was more than that. The sight of him made Stella's heart skip a beat. Romeo was even bigger than Juliet, dark gray with an imposing head.

He was this pack's alpha male, and his dominance over the other wolves was visible. While the other wolves nervously raced back and forth, Romeo sat facing the humans and calmly stared them down. His eyes shone with intelligence and confidence.

Stella was surprised to feel a shiver move up her spine. She had spent years defending wolves, telling her classmates they were nothing to fear.

And yet . . . she couldn't deny Romeo frightened her a little. He was just so *wild*. And they were about to let this kinglike creature loose in the woods. It was like adding a shot of pepper sauce to a plate of scrambled eggs. Suddenly everything was much more interesting.

Cora laughed uneasily. "He looks pretty intense."

"Probably hungry." Norma shrugged. "We last fed them four days ago."

Nina had come up to them. "Why haven't they been fed?" She had her pen poised above her notebook.

Norma smiled at her. "We're a bit concerned that the wolves won't want to leave the pen. This afternoon, we left some road-killed elk in the woods. Hopefully it will lure them out."

Mack tapped Norma's shoulder. "The photogra-

pher's ready. Want to give me a hand with the gate?"

"You bet."

Norma and Mack approached the gate and unlocked it. They pulled it back.

Stella's heart was doing a slow thud, thud. She reached for Cora's hand without taking her eyes off the wolves.

They seemed to be waiting for something. Did they think this was a trick? Did they know that the gate was open?

Suddenly, like a horse out of a starting gate, Romeo gathered himself and exploded in speed. He raced directly out into the twilight. Juliet was a dark blur behind him.

Stella gave Cora's hand a squeeze.

The wolves were free. And the world had changed forever.

LIVING WITH MOUNTAIN LIONS

Imagine standing in the woods and seeing a mountain lion slink by. Would you feel thrilled like Stella does in this story? Or frightened?

Mountain lions—also called cougars, pumas, panthers, and catamounts—are known to live in thirteen U.S. states and in Canada's Alberta and British Columbia provinces. Unconfirmed sightings in other states are common.

Have you ever seen one?

Probably not.

Most people never see a mountain lion because there just aren't that many wandering through the woods. Scientists aren't sure how many mountain lions are out there, but officials in most western states feel that the population—while small—is healthy enough to allow mountain lion hunting. Just over 1,900 mountain lions were killed by hunters in 1990, an average year.

Although 1,900 mountain lions may seem like a lot, bagging a lion isn't easy. That's because the creatures generally avoid people. Even experienced trackers can have difficulty finding one. Mountain lions move through the woods quietly. They don't meow like house cats or roar like African lions. The big cats can jump twenty feet in a single leap and run at speeds up to forty miles per hour. They can hear high-pitched sounds that humans miss. At night, they can see six times better than people can.

Catching lions is also difficult because they are almost always on the move. On average the cats claim territories—or home ranges—of around fifty square miles. From dusk to dawn, when they are most active, lions wander their territories searching for prey. They can cover up to ten miles in a single night.

Rebounding population

Although mountain lions are hard to find, more people may be seeing them soon. That's because the population of lions is growing in one of the nation's most populous states. California banned hunting mountain lions in 1972. The state is now home to an estimated 5,000 lions—about twice as many as lived there when the ban first went into effect. The mountain lion population in Montana's Yellowstone National Park also rebounded during the 1990s.

At the same time, the number of people living in California and visiting Yellowstone has grown. More mountain lions, plus more people living and playing in their habitat, could mean only one thing—more interaction between the two species. And that has led to more mountain lion attacks.

Just ask Dante Swallow. This six-year-old boy was hiking with a group of campers near Missoula, Montana, in August 1998 when he was attacked by a big male mountain lion. According to news reports, the lion's teeth punctured the boy's neck only a quarter-inch from his jugular vein. Dante was saved when his sixteen-year-old camp counselor pulled him from the lion's jaws.

Stories like Dante's set people's hearts pounding. They're printed in newspapers around the country and retold over and over again. Unfortunately that creates the impression that mountain lions love to attack humans.

Actually such attacks are extremely rare. Scientists aren't sure why these usually shy creatures sometimes decide to pounce on people. One theory says the attacking lions are starving or stressed by lack of wild places—for example, when a subdivision pops up on land they used to call home.

Another theory is that lions attack when humans unwittingly make themselves look like deer or other animals mountain lions hunt. A lion's interest may be attracted to the movement of a jogger. If the jogger then stops and leans over to tie a shoelace, the lion may see a person that's deer-shaped and looks small enough to attack. When mountain lions do attack humans, they usually choose children as their victims.

From 1890 to 1990, lions attacked only fifty-three people in the United States and Canada. Thirteen of those people died from their injuries. During the same period of time, more people died from bee stings, lightning strikes, or from hitting deer with their cars.

Prevent attacks

Most conflicts between humans and mountain lions occur in Montana; California; and British Columbia, Canada. If you live in these areas or vacation there, the following precautions should lower your chances of encountering a lion:

- **Feed animals inside.** Let your pets eat indoors. And don't feed wild animals such as deer and raccoons. Small animals may attract predators.
- **Protect livestock and pets.** Keep sheep, cows, and goats in sheds or barns at night. Bring dogs and cats into the house, or provide a kennel with a secure top.
- **Play outside during the day.** Not after dusk or before dawn.
- **Hike in groups.** Let lions know you're there by wearing bells while traveling through their habitat.
- **Keep your distance.** If you spot a mountain lion, give it a way to escape confrontation.

What to do if attacked

Dante Swallow survived because his camp counselor thought fast and fought back. Here's what you should do in the highly unlikely event that you ever meet a hungry lion that wants to turn *you* into lunch:

- **Make noise.** Lions usually flee when they realize humans are nearby.

- **Look large.** Open your jacket. Stretch out your arms.
- **Back away.** Don't run because that may stimulate the lion's instinct to chase prey.
- **Stay standing.** Crouching down may make you look more like a prey animal.
- **Throw sticks or rocks.** But don't bend over to pick them up!